Copyright © 1999 by Susanna Gretz

First U.S. edition 1999

Library of Congress Cataloging-in-Publication Data

Gretz, Susanna.
Rabbit food / Susanna Gretz.—1st U.S. ed.
p. cm.
Summary: Uncle Bunny, who has been summoned to make sure that John
joins his fellow rabbits in eating lots of vegetables,
reveals a surprising dislike for carrots.
ISBN 0-7636-0731-2
[1. Vegetables—Fiction. 2. Food habits—Fiction. 3. Rabbits—Fiction.
4. Uncles—Fiction.] I. Title.
PZ7.G8636Raag 1999
[E]—dc21   98-36110

2 4 6 8 10 9 7 5 3

Printed in Hong Kong

This book was typeset in Stempel Schneidler.
The pictures were done in watercolor.

Candlewick Press
2067 Massachusetts Avenue
Cambridge, Massachusetts 02140

RABBIT FOOD

Susanna Gretz

CANDLEWICK PRESS
CAMBRIDGE, MASSACHUSETTS

Celery, tomatoes, peas, carrots, and
mushrooms—that's rabbit food!
Danny and Debbie
love all of it.
John doesn't.
"Don't you want to grow up
big and strong?" asks his mom.

"**NO,**" says John.
"Why not?" asks Dad.
"Because grownups eat celery and
tomatoes and peas and carrots," says John,
"and worst of all, mushrooms . . ."

Yuk!

The truth is, John hardly eats any rabbit food at all.
"Maybe he's just not hungry enough," says Mom.
"Maybe Uncle Bunny can help," says Dad.

Dad makes a quick telephone call,
and the very next day . . .

Uncle Bunny arrives!
Everyone is glad
to see him.

"Now, we're off for the weekend," says Mom.
"Uncle Bunny will look after you."
"There's food in the kitchen," says Dad,
"and please see that John eats some of everything."

"No problem," says Uncle Bunny.

At lunchtime John builds a bridge
with his celery, tomatoes, and carrots.
"Eat up," says Uncle Bunny. "They're delicious!"
"Yuk," says John.
"Eat your rabbit food, and you'll grow big and
strong like me," says Uncle Bunny.
But when no one is looking . . .

Uncle Bunny
hides his carrots
under his
napkin.

At supper John makes a cave with his toast, and
he hides his peas and mushrooms underneath.
"Try some," says Uncle Bunny.
"Just one teeny tiny bite. They're good for you."
"Yuk!" says John.
"Eat your rabbit food and you'll grow big and
strong like me!" says Uncle Bunny.
But when no one is looking . . .

Uncle Bunny hides his carrots in
the flowerpot.

Next
morning
they all
play
soccer . . .

then
bunny
jump . . .

then
tug of war.

They get quite hungry.
Everyone, even John, digs into Sunday lunch.
It's baked potato rabbits: the eyes are peas,
the noses are mushrooms, the mouths are pieces of tomato,
the whiskers are pieces of celery, and the ears are carrots . . .
that is, all except for Uncle Bunny's rabbit.
"Why doesn't **your** rabbit have ears,
Uncle Bunny?" asks John.

Uncle Bunny doesn't seem to hear.
"Hurry up and eat," he says. "We're off to
climb a mountain this afternoon!"

Debbie reaches the mountaintop first.

That evening, everyone is **very** hungry.
Uncle Bunny puts what's left of the food on the table,
but first he wants to watch the news.
"Help yourselves,"
he tells the little rabbits.
John is so hungry,
he eats lots of everything.

Now Uncle Bunny wants some food, too.
But there's not a scrap left on the table.
All that's left in the kitchen is a bunch of carrots.
"You don't like carrots, do you, Uncle?" says John.

"Well, I, uh . . . **no**," says Uncle Bunny.

"But they're delicious!"
yells John, and everyone jumps
on Uncle Bunny.

"They're good for you!
Just *try* a little! Just one teeny tiny
bite . . . and you'll grow
BIG and **STRONG** like **US!**"

Uncle Bunny bites off a
very tiny piece of carrot.
He chews it very slowly.
Then he bites off another
tiny piece . . . and another.

Just then Mom and Dad appear.
"I did the best jump!" Danny tells them.
"I climbed the mountain first!" says Debbie.
"I ate celery and tomatoes and carrots and peas," says John,
"and **MUSHROOMS!**"

Mom and Dad are delighted.
"However did you do it, Uncle Bunny?" says Dad.
"You're terrific," says Mom.
Uncle Bunny doesn't answer, because his mouth is full of carrots.

"In fact," he says at last . . .
"they're not bad."

DATE			